the Ant and the Grasshopper

Based on a story by Aesop

Retold by
Katie Daynes

Illustrated by
Merel Eyckerman

Reading consultant: Alison Kelly
Roehampton University

Grasshopper
sings in the sun.

Ant works.

"Play with me,"
says Grasshopper.

6

"I can't," says Ant.

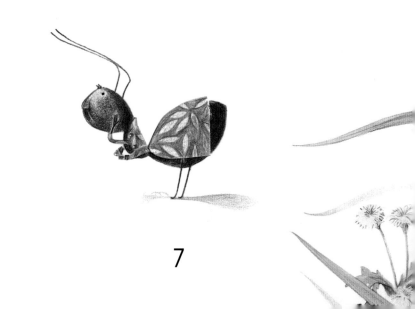

"Winter will come,"
says Ant.

10

"And you will
be hungry."

Grasshopper laughs
and sings.

Ant carries more corn.

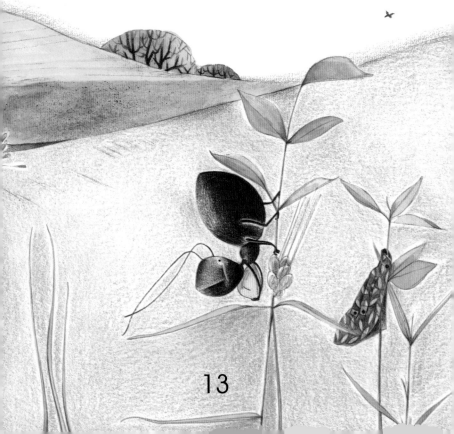

Winter comes.

Ant is happy.

Grasshopper is cold...

...and very hungry.

"Come inside," says Ant.

"Thank you," says
Grasshopper.

22

"Next summer
I'll work too."

23

Puzzles

Puzzle 1

What is Grasshopper doing?
Match the words to
the pictures.

A

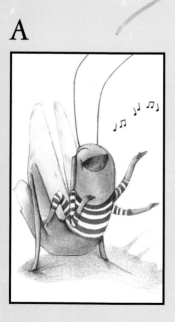

B

feeling cold singing

resting talking

C

D

Puzzle 2

Help Grasshopper spot
the differences. There are
six to find.

Puzzle 3

Choose the best sentence in each picture.

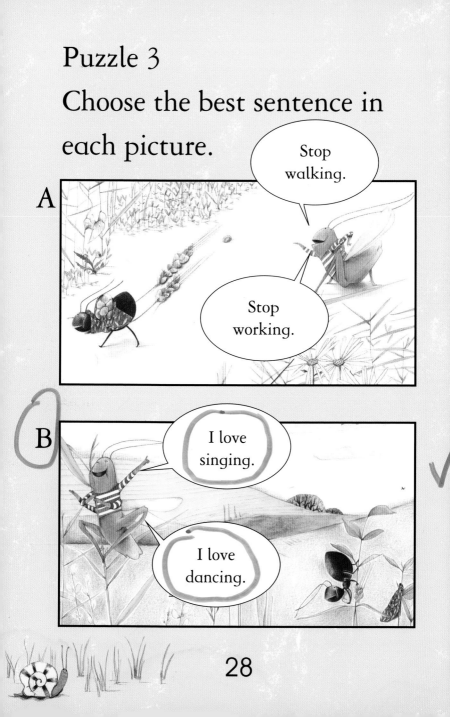

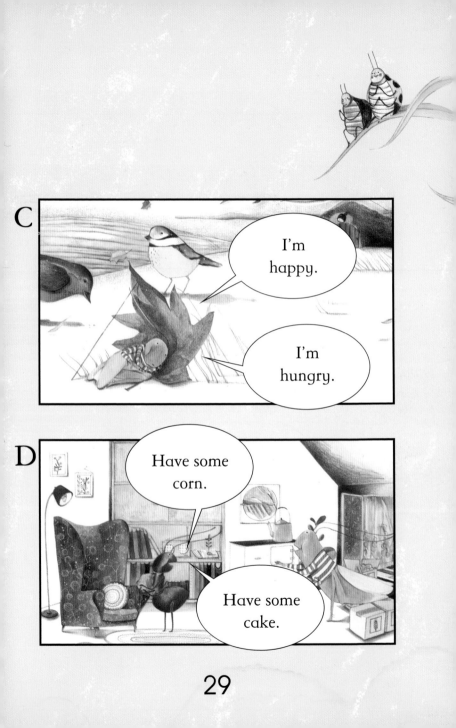

Answers to puzzles

Puzzle 1

A

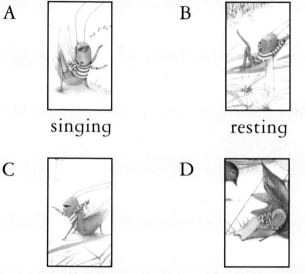

singing

B

resting

C

talking

D

feeling cold

Puzzle 2

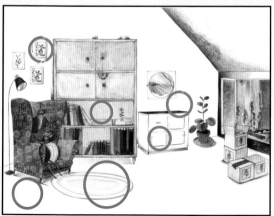

Puzzle 3

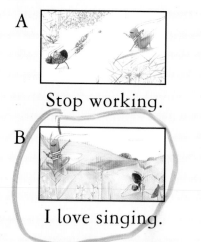

A
Stop working.

B
I love singing.

C
I'm hungry.

D
Have some corn.

About the story

The Ant and the Grasshopper is one of Aesop's Fables, a collection of stories first told in Ancient Greece around 4,000 years ago. The stories always have a "moral" (a message or lesson) at the end. In this story, Grasshopper learns that it is best to be prepared.

31

Designed by Abigail Brown
Series editor: Lesley Sims
Series designer: Russell Punter

First published in 2008 by Usborne Publishing Ltd., Usborne House,
83-85 Saffron Hill, London EC1N 8RT, England. www.usborne.com
Copyright © 2008 Usborne Publishing Ltd.